BRATZ™

Rock Angelz™

Ready to Rock!

GROSSET & DUNLAP
Published by the Penguin Group
Penguin Group (USA) Inc., 375 Hudson Street, New York, New York 10014, U.S.A.
Penguin Group (Canada), 10 Alcorn Avenue, Toronto, Ontario, Canada M4V 3B2
(a division of Pearson Penguin Canada Inc.)
Penguin Books Ltd, 80 Strand, London WC2R 0RL, England
Penguin Ireland, 25 St Stephen's Green, Dublin 2, Ireland
(a division of Penguin Books Ltd)
Penguin Group (Australia), 250 Camberwell Road, Camberwell, Victoria 3124, Australia
(a division of Pearson Australia Group Pty Ltd)
Penguin Books India Pvt Ltd, 11 Community Centre, Panchsheel Park, New Delhi
110 017, India
Penguin Group (NZ), Cnr Airborne and Rosedale Roads, Albany, Auckland 1310,
New Zealand (a division of Pearson New Zealand Ltd)
Penguin Books (South Africa) (Pty) Ltd, 24 Sturdee Avenue, Rosebank,
Johannesburg 2196, South Africa

Penguin Books Ltd, Registered Offices:
80 Strand, London WC2R 0RL, England

Used under license by Penguin Young Readers Group. Published in 2005 by Grosset & Dunlap, a division of Penguin Young Readers Group, 345 Hudson Street, New York, New York 10014. GROSSET & DUNLAP is a trademark of Penguin Group (USA) Inc. Printed in the U.S.A.

Library of Congress Control Number: 2005011440

ISBN 0-448-44008-3   10 9 8 7 6 5 4 3 2 1

By Sierra Harimann

Based on the screenplay by Peggy Nicoll

Grosset & Dunlap

Behind the Scenes at: Bratz Mag

Hey! Thanks for picking up the first-ever issue of *Bratz Magazine*! We are so totally psyched to have you as a reader. Just wait till you check out all the incredible, funkadelic stuff that's packed inside this month's issue—from "Angel's Angelic Beauty Tips" to "Bunny Boo's Beats," we have got a *lot* in store for you!

You may be wondering how the girls with a passion for fashion decided to start our very own stylin' magazine. Or maybe you're curious to know how we managed to become rock stars overnight. (That's totally us on the cover—the *Bratz Rock Angelz* currently have the #1 hit on the radio!) Well, it's an awesome story that we'll pack into this premiere issue, along with all the other fun stuff we know you love.

So kick back and get ready for a rockin' first issue of *Bratz Mag*! Write us some letters and let us know what ya think!

Lotsa Luv,
Jade, Cloe, Sasha, and Yasmin
The Editors

Chapter One

"Ooooh, listen to my horoscope," Cloe said between sips of her strawberry-banana smoothie. "It says I'm way outgoing, a great friend to all my pals, *and* that I'm gonna meet a handsome prince who will carry me off into the sunset on his horse!"

Her friend Sasha grabbed the magazine out of Cloe's hands.

"Right, Angel," Sasha said teasingly. "A horse is *totally* realistic."

"You never know," Cloe retorted. It was true that the horse thing wasn't very realistic, but she thought the rest of her horoscope sounded amazingly accurate. After all, she was a super romantic at heart. And she *was* incredibly outgoing—her sweet, easy-going nature was the reason her best friends Sasha, Yasmin, and Jade had given her the nickname Angel.

The girls had been best friends for ages, and they

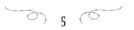

knew one another so well that each girl had a nickname based on her personality. Sasha was known as Bunny Boo because she was so into the hip-hop scene. Jade was the Kool Kat of the crew. With her slammin' sense of style, she was able to pull off fashions the other girls only dreamed of!

Yasmin was the newest member of the foursome. When she first started attending Stiles High with Cloe, Sasha, and Jade, she was supershy. But once the other girls got to know her, they realized how great she was, and they dubbed her their Pretty Princess.

Despite their different personalities, the girls were practically inseparable, and everyone at Stiles High knew that when one girl was around, the others weren't far behind.

"It also says you're a major drama queen," Sasha continued reading from Cloe's horoscope.

"That is *sooo* untrue," Cloe said with a pout. "Ah . . . ah . . . ah . . . *ACHOO!*" She clutched her heart and gasped. "You guys! I think I just had an out-of-the-blue arterial explosion!"

Yasmin and Sasha couldn't help but laugh.

"What's so funny?" Cloe asked, completely unaware. "What did I do?"

Yasmin leaned over to check out the magazine. "Nothing, drama queen," she teased Cloe.

"Well, mine says I'm strong, sensitive, and a little secretive," Yasmin read aloud. "And there's a mysterious guy in my future who will change my life."

Just at that moment, the girls' friend Eitan brought Yasmin the triple-berry smoothie she had ordered from the juice bar. He was working there part-time to raise money for a new guitar.

"Here ya go, Yaz," Eitan said, giving her a big smile. Sasha looked over at Yasmin and raised her eyebrows.

"A mysterious guy," Sasha mouthed silently to Yasmin, who quickly dug her elbow into Sasha's side.

"Thanks, Eitan," Yasmin said, ignoring Sasha.

"Catch ya later, girls," Eitan replied as he headed back to work.

Sasha turned her attention back to the magazine. "Check this out," she began. "It says music is my thing and my style is off the hook. I can't commit to any one guy, but when I'm this gorgeous, why should I? And I'm a—"

Sasha closed the magazine abruptly, annoyed. "Yeah, right. Like they know what they're talking about."

Cloe grabbed the magazine back. "Let me see that," she said.

"'A control freak!'" Cloe read, picking up where Sasha had left off. "Wow, Bunny Boo! That's practically psychic."

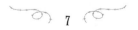

Cloe jabbed Sasha playfully in the arm. "Just teasing!" Cloe added. "That's part of the reason why you have such amazing organizational skills."

Before Sasha could respond, the girls' friend Jade came running over to their table at the juice bar.

"I got it! I got it!" Jade shrieked.

"You mean the latest Crash CD?" Yasmin asked.

Jade picked up the magazine the girls had been reading and proudly displayed it.

"Better!" she said. "I got the student internship!"

"The one at *Your Thing* magazine?" Yasmin gasped.

Jade nodded. "You are looking at the new intern for Ms. Burdine Maxwell, editor-in-chief."

"Rockin'!" Cloe cried, giving Jade a huge hug.

"Awesome!" Sasha added. "That fashion-challenged magazine needs someone fashion-forward like you."

Sasha scooted over so Jade could squeeze into the booth with her friends.

"Wow, Jade," Cloe said excitedly. "Will you get to go to all the runway shows?"

"And watch all the supermodel meltdowns?" Yasmin added.

"And get free passes to all the happening concerts?" Sasha asked.

"I sure hope so," Jade said. "It's totally my biggest dream, and it's coming true!"

Suddenly something caught Sasha's eye. She groaned.

"Nine-one-one!" she told her friends. "Mean girl alert at two o'clock!"

The girls turned to see Kirstee and Kaycee, two of the nastiest girls at Stiles High, approaching. Kaycee could be spotted from a mile away thanks to the white bandage she wore over her nose, a remnant of her latest nose job. The girls were twin sisters, and their evil antics had earned them the nickname the Tweevils among everyone else at Stiles High. Kirstee was definitely smarter and meaner than her sister Kaycee, and she was usually the one who came up with the Tweevils' mean schemes. Their idea of fashion included all the trends from the previous year, as well as *lots* of pink.

"Well, look who's here," Kirstee said menacingly.

"The fashion freaks," Kaycee added, shooting the girls a nasty look.

"Whatever," Jade said, trying her best to ignore them.

"Whatever," Kirstee and Kaycee mimicked back sarcastically as they walked past the girls' table.

"Yo, Cloe," Yasmin said. "I spy your Prince Charming!"

The girls' friends Cameron and Dylan rolled into the juice bar on their skateboards. Cloe's eyes immediately

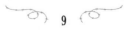

went to supersweet but shy Cameron. Cloe had been friends with him for years, and everyone knew that Cameron had a thing for Cloe, though neither of them would ever admit it.

As the boys skated toward the girls, Dylan started showing off with some fancy tricks and turns. Right as he was spinning into a turn, Kirstee and Kaycee walked past the boys with smoothies in hand.

"Check this out," Dylan bragged as he tipped his board up and wheeled around.

"Dylan!" Cloe shouted. "Watch out!"

But it was too late! Dylan skidded off the board and slammed right into Kaycee, whose drink went flying into the air . . . and landed all over the front of Kirstee's tailored pink dress.

"Owwwwww!" Kaycee howled as the skateboard hit her in the nose.

"My new ensemble!" Kirstee shrieked in a fake French accent.

Cloe got up and walked over to the Tweevils.

"Are you guys okay?" she asked sweetly.

Kirstee totally ignored her sister's howls of pain. Instead she snapped back at Cloe, "In case you didn't notice, my outfit is, like, *totally* trashed!"

"Don't freak," Dylan said smoothly. "It was an accident."

"Don't tell me not to freak, you, you, *skater boy*!" Kirstee retorted. She grabbed Kaycee, who was still muttering in pain, and the two stormed off.

Dylan turned back to his friends. "Rewind?" he asked.

"Go for it!" Cloe said.

Dylan skated a few feet, jumped off the board, did a twist, and landed perfectly on the board.

"Sweet!" Sasha said.

"Can I try?" Cloe asked.

"Are you sure you can handle it?" Dylan retorted. He looked skeptical.

Cloe didn't respond. She just grabbed the skateboard, skated a few feet in front of her, and launched into the air. She twisted, landing on the ground on top of the board, which had stayed under her feet the entire time.

"Awesome moves, Cloe," Cameron said, visibly impressed.

"Thanks, Cameron," Cloe responded coyly. "I've got a lot of cool moves."

Cameron raised his eyebrows at her, and Cloe turned the same shade of red as her Juicy Apple lip gloss.

"I mean, on the skateboard," she added. "You know, ollies, donkey kicks, seven-twenties, stuff like that."

Cameron smiled at her. "Do you think you could

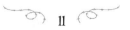

teach me a seven-twenty sometime?"

"Yeah, sure. Whatever," Cloe responded.

"Hey, guys. Did you hear?" Yasmin interjected. "Jade is gonna be working at *Your Thing* magazine for the whole summer!"

"That's tight," Cameron said with an approving nod.

"Awesome!" Dylan chimed in. "What's *Your Thing*?"

Sasha threw the magazine at him. "Boys!" she said with a sigh. "They can be so clueless!"

Chapter Two

The following Monday, Jade spent longer than usual putting her outfit together. It was the first day of her internship at *Your Thing*, and she just *had* to look amazing! She dug through her closet until she found the perfect outfit and matching accessories.

"Now that's stylin'!" Jade said to herself as she put the finishing touches on her clothes and makeup and took one last look in the mirror. She grabbed her tote bag, which was full of copies of *Your Thing*, a zebra-print fur-covered notebook, and her fave glitter gel pen, and headed out the door.

Half an hour later, Jade stood nervously in front of Burdine Maxwell's desk, looking at the back of Burdine's enormous desk chair.

"Do you know who you are talking to?" Burdine barked into the phone. "I am the founder, president, editor-in-chief, and Queen of Fashion, you ridiculous, incompetent moron! I want a dozen pairs of those size-eleven peony pink pumps here tomorrow. And *don't* give me any more of your lame excuses that you don't make them in my size!"

Burdine slammed the phone down and spun around in her chair.

"Mother of pink!" she shrieked, startled to find Jade standing there. She took in Jade's outfit and her mouth twisted into a sour smile. Burdine adjusted the rhinestone tiara on her head.

"Well, well, well," she said. "What are you supposed to be?"

"I'm Jade, your new student intern," Jade responded, trying for her cheeriest and most pleasant voice. "And I just want to tell you that I am so totally psyched to be working here with you on *Your Thing*. I've got a ton of ideas for the magazine—"

"Oh, really?" Burdine interrupted as she drummed her manicured peony pink nails menacingly on the desk. "Do share."

"Well, I was thinking that maybe we could do a column on street trends. You know, see what's taking off at clubs, and do a quiz fest—"

"Stop!" Burdine barked, holding out her hand like a traffic cop. "Just so we understand each other . . . *I* come up with the ideas. *Your Thing* is my magazine. You work for me, and your title is . . . *nothing*."

"I'm sorry," Jade stammered. "I didn't mean to—"

The door chime cut her off. Jade turned to see Kirstee and Kaycee stride into the office wearing identical plaid suits and carrying a pink box with an enormous pink bow.

"Ah, my other interns," Burdine cooed. "Two lovely girls."

She eyed the gift. "Ah, pink. My favorite color!"

Burdine walked over to the computer and punched a key. A long ream of paper spewed out of the attached printer. Burdine ripped the sheets off and handed the papers to Jade.

"Here's your first assignment," she said. Then she turned back to her desk and scribbled something quickly on a pink Post-It.

"And here's what I want you girls to do," she said as she handed the tiny note to Kirstee and Kaycee.

As Jade was going over her long list of tasks, a timer chimed. Burdine glanced at the clock.

"Now get busy, girls," she told them. "Royale and I have some shoe shopping to do."

Royale was Burdine's yappy little dog. Burdine scooped him up from the pink velvet cushion at her feet and tucked him into her pink handbag. Then she strode out the door.

Kaycee looked at the pink Post-It in her hand. "Neato," she said as she grabbed the camera off of Burdine's desk. "It's a fashion assignment. I need you guys to model for me."

"Well, okay," Jade said hesitantly as she struck a pose. Kirstee immediately stepped into the photo in front of Jade, blocking the camera. She grinned at her sister as she switched from one pose to the next. Kaycee snapped away, coaxing Kirstee in a syrupy voice.

"That's it, Kirstee," she said. "Beautiful. Yeah. Give me a supermodel smile. Gorgeous! Now let me see a little pout. That was great. Okay, now it's Jade's turn."

Just as Jade was about to strike her best pose, Kaycee snapped the shot.

"Wait a sec," Jade said, flustered. "I wasn't ready yet!"

Kaycee completely ignored Jade's remark as she studied the shot on the digital camera screen.

"Perfection," Kaycee said.

Kirstee flopped dramatically onto the overstuffed floral print sofa and threw her arm across her forehead.

"Wooh!" she said unconvincingly. "I'm just exhausted from all that work!"

Kaycee snickered in agreement as she grabbed a stack of fashion magazines off Burdine's desk and squeezed herself onto the couch next to Kirstee.

"Shove over, Kirstee," she said, bumping her sister's hip with her own. "You're totally hogging the whole thing." She put her feet up and opened her copy of *Your Thing*.

As the twins flipped through the magazines, Jade looked over her list.

"Vacuum carpets and curtains, water plants, dust desk and furniture . . ." Jade read. "Wow! This is a lot for one person. Maybe you guys could help me out?"

Jade looked over at the twins, who were still busy relaxing on the sofa.

"Sorry," Kirstee replied without looking up from her magazine. "N.O.P."

"N.O.P.?" Jade asked, puzzled.

"Not our problem," Kaycee and Kirstee recited in unison.

Jade sighed. This day was not turning out how she had planned. First Burdine was totally rude to her, then the Tweevils showed up, and now *this*. She looked down at the list again. After she was finished cleaning the entire office, she was supposed to steam-clean Burdine's entire closet full of pink suits. *Well, I'd better get to work*, she thought to herself as she glanced at the Tweevils yapping on their cell phones.

Jade started vacuuming the carpets and then moved

on to the curtains. Next she watered all the plants in the office, repeatedly lugging the full watering can from the sink all the way across the room. Then Jade moved on to Burdine's desk, where she had been instructed to sort and file all of Burdine's papers. As she was sorting and stacking, the Tweevils pulled out nail polish and started buffing and polishing their nails.

Jade had managed to stack all of Burdine's papers into neat little piles, and she was about to begin filing when Kirstee pulled out a miniature nail fan. Jade saw Kirstee reaching for the switch and she leaped out in front of the fan.

"Nooooo!" Jade cried, but it was too late. Kirstee flipped the switch on the fan and the papers went up in a huge *whoosh*!

"Oh, did I do that?" Kirstee said innocently. "Sorry!"

Jade was about to come back with a snappy retort, but she held her tongue. *Those nasty, conniving Tweevils aren't worth it*, she reminded herself as she moved on to Burdine's closet to steam-clean the suits. Meanwhile, Kirstee and Kaycee were busy gossiping about the Queen of Pink.

"Can you believe Burdine?" Kirstee asked. "Everything about her is, like, sooo plastic."

"Totally," Kaycee retorted. "She reminds me of that

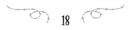

fashion doll you used to hit me with when we were three."

The door chimed and Burdine entered carrying a shopping bag full of shoes. Royale trailed behind her, pink rhinestone-studded leash in his mouth and tail wagging. Kaycee and Kirstee raced over to the computer as Burdine flopped down in her chair.

"Okay, girls," Burdine said. "Show me the 'Fashion Dos and Don'ts' assignment."

Kaycee clicked the mouse to reveal a photo of Kirstee grinning overzealously at the camera. "Okay, this is a *do*," Kaycee said. Then she clicked the mouse again to reveal a picture of Jade. "And *this* is a *don't*."

Jade gasped.

"Perfection!" Burdine squealed with delight.

"Um . . . excuse me," Jade said, her face turning red. "I have to use the bathroom."

As soon as Jade got into the bathroom, tears started streaming down her face. She looked in the mirror. "Maybe they're right," she said softly to herself. "I'm nothing but one big fashion don't."

She took out her cell and dialed Cloe.

"Kool Kat!" Cloe answered. Jade's friends had given her that nickname because they didn't know of a single

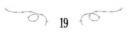

person on Earth who was cooler than her. "How's it going?"

"Totally terrible, Angel," Jade said sadly. "Burdine is so mean, and she really hates me. And you won't believe who I have to work with—the Tweevils!"

Cloe gasped in horror. "Wow, Jade. That's really awful, but try to hang in there. This is your dream, remember?"

"It's more like a nightmare right now!" Jade replied. "But you're right. This is my dream, and I have to stick it out. You're such a good friend, Angel. Thanks."

"No problem, Kool Kat," Cloe said. "I'll check in with you later."

Jade hung up the phone. She felt better already—that is, until she caught a glimpse in the mirror of Kirstee and Kaycee standing right behind her.

"Oh, Burdine is such a meanie-weanie," Kirstee said in a squeaky, high-pitched baby voice.

"And Kirstee and Kaycee are so nasty-wasty!" Kaycee chimed in.

Jade's face turned pink as she rushed out of the bathroom and back to the Queen of Pink herself. Jade found Burdine surrounded by boxes of shoes from her shopping spree. She was apparently trying them all on again.

"There you are!" Burdine snapped at Jade. "Now,

where's my mail?"

Jade picked up a stack of invitations from the corner of Burdine's desk. "It's right here," she replied. "You have some really rockin' invitations here. Look! There's one from that cool new teen fashion store, and another from—"

Burdine grabbed the envelopes out of Jade's hands. She flicked the first invitation onto the floor, followed by the next, and the one after that.

"Junk. Junk! JUNK!" Burdine said as she tossed each invite aside. "More junk! Mother of pink! Don't you know junk mail when you see it, you silly girl?!"

As Jade bent down to scoop up the invitations, Burdine tossed a pair of pink pumps onto the floor beside her.

"I'm wearing my new pumps today, so get these old ones polished. And where is my lunch already? 'Get Burdine's lunch' was number twenty-seven on your list!"

"But I don't even know wh—" The ringing telephone cut Jade off.

"Hello?" Burdine said into the phone. "What do you mean sales of *Your Thing* have dropped? That's impossible!"

"—what you eat for lunch," Jade finished her question, but Burdine had turned away to shout at the caller on

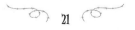

the other end of the phone.

Jade turned to Kirstee and Kaycee. "Um, do you guys know what Burdine likes for lunch?" she asked.

"Sure," Kirstee answered. "We'll phone in the order."

"But it's your turn to pick it up at the deli," Kaycee added.

"Okay," Jade replied. "I guess I'll have to get to these shoes later." She tossed the pumps and the junk mail into her bag and headed out to pick up Burdine's lunch.

Jade returned half an hour later to find Burdine at her desk putting on lipstick while the Tweevils pretended to be busy faxing and filing papers.

"Here's your lunch," Jade said, handing Burdine a large brown paper bag. "I got your usual—"

Burdine shrieked as she opened the bag, which contained a giant cheeseburger.

"Mother of pink!" she shouted, recoiling from the bag in horror. "What *is* that thing?" She knocked the cheeseburger onto the floor and Royale went after it voraciously.

"It's your lunch," Jade answered. "I thought that's what you liked."

"Carbs?!" Burdine yelled, clutching her chest. "What

are you trying to do . . . kill me? I only eat greens!"

"But—" Jade tried to protest, but Burdine cut her off.

"Spare me your excuses! You are fired. Do you hear me? FIRED!"

Burdine started moving toward Jade, knocking things off her desk as she went.

"And not only will you never, ever work at this magazine again, but you will never, ever work ay any magazine in the whole world," Burdine's eyes bulged and the veins in her neck stood out as she screamed at Jade. It was not an attractive look. "Am I making myself clear?" Burdine continued. "You are fired for life! In fact, even your children and grandchildren are fired. Fired! FIRED!"

Jade stared at Burdine and at the snickering Tweevils in horror. She grabbed her bag and turned to leave. *My life is so over*, she thought to herself as she fled out the door.

Chapter Three

Later that afternoon, Cloe, Yasmin, and Sasha were perched next to Jade on her bed, consoling her.

"It's so unfair," Jade sniffled. "All of my hopes and dreams were, like, totally destroyed in just three hours!"

"Don't worry, Kool Kat," Cloe told her friend comfortingly. "Everything will work out. You have way too much talent to not make it."

"Yeah, Jade," Yasmin chimed in. "You're a fashion superhero. Burdine's the one who's majorly clueless, not you."

"You guys really think so?" Jade asked her friends, her jet-black eyes damp and wide with disbelief.

"Of course!" Yasmin affirmed.

"Totally," Cloe said.

"And we are *never* wrong when it comes to fashion!" Sasha piped up. She smiled at Jade warmly. "Now come on, people! It's time for some serious cheering-up."

All four girls said in unison: "Shopping!"

Jade, Sasha, Cloe, and Yasmin emerged from the last store for the day carrying bags full of the latest, hottest fashions.

"Thanks, guys," Jade said to her friends. "You are the best for being there for me."

"No prob," said Cloe.

"Yeah, anytime!" Sasha said.

"That's what best friends are for," Yasmin wisely added.

"Ugh! Girlfriend nine-one-one!" Sasha said as she caught a glimpse of the Tweevils emerging from Pretty 'N' Pink laden with pink shopping bags. "Major eyesores straight ahead."

"Well, well, well," Kirstee said with a smirk as she and Kaycee approached the other girls. "If it isn't Jade and her little band of fashion faux pas."

"Oh, *parlez-vous français*?" Yasmin asked.

Kirstee shot Yasmin a withering look. "Oui . . . duh!" Then she turned to Jade. "So, Jade, what are you going to do now that your career in fashion is over?"

"Her career in fashion isn't over," Sasha interjected. "It's just beginning."

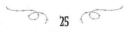

"Oh, really?" Kirstee shot back. "As what? A fast-food delivery girl?"

At that, the Tweevils spun around and walked off, snickering to themselves.

"Those fashion disasters are *pathetic*," Sasha said. "Come on, girls! Let's hit the juice bar!"

A few minutes later, the girls were sitting in their favorite corner booth at the juice bar. Someone had left a copy of *Your Thing* magazine on the table. Sasha picked it up and started thumbing through the pages.

"Kool Kat, you wouldn't have learned a thing at this lame-o magazine. I mean, just look at this layout! It's so poorly organized. This sidebar should be over here, and the colors are all totally wrong!"

"You're right," Jade replied. "That magazine is *so* yesterday!"

"Ya know," Yasmin said thoughtfully, playing with a strand of her chocolate-brown locks. "We should really have our own magazine."

Sasha gasped. "Pretty Princess, that is a scorchin' idea! I don't know why none of us thought of it before."

"It is?" Yasmin asked.

"Totally!" Cloe interjected excitedly. "I could write an advice column. It would be called 'Dear Cloe,' and I would respond to people's fashion emergencies. I can totally see the first question: 'What should I wear on my first date?' "

"And I could write about trends," Yasmin said as she twisted herself into a yoga pose. "Where to hang, where to work it, and where to learn the latest poses!"

Suddenly, Sasha jumped onto the table and started dancing to the hip-hop music that was playing on the juice bar radio. "And I could be the editor!" Sasha shouted with a swish of her hips.

Jade rolled her eyes and Cloe and Yasmin shot Sasha a look, their hands on their hips.

"Bunny Boo!" her friends scolded in unison.

"I mean, the *music* editor," Sasha continued. "I'd review what's down and slammin' and what gets everybody jammin'!"

Jade jumped up from the table and strutted down the juice bar aisle. She did a fancy turn and then turned to face her friends, striking an awesome supermodel pose.

"And I'll be the most cutting-edge—"

"FASHION EDITOR!" her friends chimed in all at once. They looked at one another and started giggling.

Then Sasha got serious. "Wait a sec, guys," she said. "Are you all thinking what I'm thinking?"

"If you're thinking that this is the best idea since the halter top, I am *so* thinking what you're thinking." Jade responded.

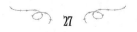

"Let's totally do it," Cloe said. "Let's start our own fashion magazine!"

The girls screamed and did a group high five.

"Wait a sec!" Cloe said. "Reality check: What about an office? There's no way we can afford one. I'll have to babysit every night . . . even on weekends . . . all summer long!"

"Chill, Angel," Sasha said. "Let me work on it."

The next day, the girls hopped into Sasha's car and headed across town to check out the office space Sasha had read about in a classified ad.

"The ad said the place needed a little work, but that's why the rent is so low," Sasha told her friends confidently.

They pulled up in front of a swanky office building.

"Here we are!" Sasha said.

"Love it!" Cloe said.

"Feel it!" Yasmin added.

"Hate it," Jade said glumly.

"Huh?" Cloe asked.

"It's Burdine's building," Jade responded. "If she sees me, I'm more than dead."

"Chill, Kool Kat," Sasha said. "We've got your back."

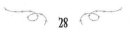

The girls headed inside and made their way to the elevators.

"Okay," Sasha said. "We're heading to the tenth floor."

The elevator stopped on three and the doors opened. Burdine and Royale got on, but Burdine was too busy yapping on her cell to notice the girls.

Jade quickly ducked behind Cloe. "Burdine," she mouthed silently to her friends.

Royale sniffed around Cloe's leg and, discovering Jade's foot, began barking voraciously.

"Hush, Royale!" Burdine snapped. "Mommy's on the phone."

On the seventh floor, the doors opened again, and Burdine and Royale exited the elevator.

Jade breathed a huge sigh of relief. "I'm so glad she's gone!"

"What's with the crown thing?" Cloe asked.

"Burdine likes to think of herself as the reigning queen of fashion," Jade replied.

"More like the queen of mean," Yasmin added.

"Well, Miss Queen Burdine is about to get what she deserves," Sasha said, a mischievous glint in her eye. "She's going head to head with the most stylin' four girls around!"

"This is it!" Yasmin announced as the elevator arrived

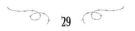

at the tenth floor. The girls stepped out into the hallway and Sasha took the lead. She stopped in front of the door at the very end of the hallway.

"'Kay, guys," Sasha said. "get ready to feast your eyes on the most totally slammin' loft in all of downtown!"

She threw the door open with an enormous flourish.

"Ta-DA!" she shouted.

"Ahhhh!" Cloe screamed. "A rat!" She jumped back as a big furry rodent scurried out the door.

"This is it?" Yasmin asked in disbelief.

The girls stood in the doorway of the most run-down space they had ever seen in their lives. Paint was peeling off the walls in huge chunks, pieces of the floorboard were missing, and the windows were streaked with layers of grime. The few pieces of furniture in the space were broken and covered in what looked like five years' worth of dust and cobwebs.

"Sasha, you can't be serious," Jade said, turning to her friend.

"Okay, so the place needs a little makeover," Sasha replied.

Jade shot her a withering look.

"Okay, a *serious* makeover," Sasha admitted. "But it's nothing we girls can't handle, right?"

Meanwhile, Cloe was having a panic attack. "What

are we going to do?" she shrieked. "This place is so beyond help! Our hopes, our dreams . . . they're completely shattered!"

"Yo, drama mama!" Sasha snapped her fingers in front of Cloe's face. "Snap out of it! We survived middle school! We can survive this."

Jade surveyed the space and twirled a piece of her jet-black hair.

"Hmmm," she mused. "A little paint, some new shelves, a computer bank, and a little dramatic flair, and I think we can make this place work!"

Sasha plunked down the boom box she was carrying and flicked it on.

"Let's hit it, girls!" she exclaimed.

Yasmin and Cloe headed to the hardware store to pick up some cleaning supplies and paint. By the time they returned with three huge cans of True Blue Hue, Sasha and Jade had already enlisted Cameron and Dylan's help. The boys were busy carrying chairs in while Sasha and Jade were draping a large red sheet over the couch and tying it on with huge pink ribbons.

"Hey, Cameron," Cloe said shyly as she laid out a drop cloth to protect the floor from paint splashes.

"Need help painting?" Cameron asked.

"Sure!" Cloe responded. "That would be great!"

The two began painting with huge rollers as Jade and

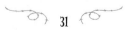

Sasha buffed the floors and waxed some tabletops. In a few hours, the office had been completely transformed. The girls had hung lamps from the ceiling and had added comfy couches and chairs all over the space. There was a drawing table and a table with four chairs for important magazine-planning meetings. The group had even installed shelves to hold shoes, clothes, and other fashion accessories that they would be photographing for the magazine. The girls slumped onto one of the couches, exhausted.

"Girls, is this place superstylin' or what?" Sasha asked.

"If your magazine is half as good as your office, it's gonna be great!" Cameron said encouragingly.

"Thanks, Cameron," Cloe said. "It does look really awesome."

"No sweat," Cameron replied. "Happy to help."

Dylan offered his help, as well. "Hey," he told the girls. "If you need me to attend any parties with supermodels, my cell's on twenty-four/seven!"

"Good-bye, Dylan!" the girls chimed together.

As soon as the boys had gone, the girls began unpacking a few boxes. Cloe opened one box and immediately let out a yelp.

"Ewwwww!" she shrieked.

"It's not another rat, is it?" Jade asked.

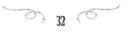

"It's worse," Cloe groaned. "Much, much worse!"

She lifted a hideous pink pump out of the box, holding it between two fingers as if it was a smelly old sock. Sasha flung her arm over her eyes in dismay.

"Puh-*lease*, Cloe!" Sasha said. "You could have at least warned us!"

Yasmin picked up the second shoe and examined it as though she were an archeologist unearthing a rare fossil. "Interesting artifact," she said. "They're probably circa 1988."

"This has got to be Dylan's totally twisted idea of a joke," Cloe said.

"Actually, they're Burdine's totally twisted idea of fashion," Jade said. "She gave them to me to have polished before she fired me, and I forgot to give them back."

Jade picked them up and shoved them into a drawer, slamming it shut.

"At least we'll never show anything that vomiticious in our magazine," Cloe said.

"You losers are starting a magazine?" a familiar voice piped in.

The girls turned to find Kaycee and Kirstee hovering in the doorway of their new office space.

"What's it about?" Kaycee asked with a smirk. "How to be a loser?"

"No, it's nothing you guys would be interested in," Cloe retorted. "It's a fashion magazine."

"Fashion?" Kirstee sneered. "With the way you spazzes dress?"

"What are you gonna call it?" Kaycee asked with a chuckle. "*Teen Hurl*?"

Kaycee and Kirstee started laughing so hard, Cloe was sure she heard Kirstee snort.

"Just wait till Burdine finds out you guys are trying to rip off *Your Thing*," Kirstee said. "She's gonna be furious."

"Get real," said Sasha. "Our thing won't be anything like *Your Thing*."

"Except that they'll both be printed on paper," Yasmin added.

"Well, Jade," Kirstee said, "sorry we won't be around to make you get fired in less than a day. But I'm sure you'll mess things up all be yourself."

"Yeah, you will," said Kaycee. "And then you'll have to fire one another."

Kirstee gave her sister a high five. "Good one, Kaycee!"

Sasha cleared her throat. "Excuse us, but we have work to do."

"And you have dry-cleaning to do," added Yasmin.

"Excuse me?" Kaycee sneered.

"The wet paint?" Jade said.

Kaycee leapt forward from where she had been standing against the doorway. There was a big blue stripe running down the back of her dress.

"You brats!" she shrieked. "You set me up!"

"Come on, Kaycee," Kirstee said. "Let's get out of here before they do something to *me*."

"I never want to see those girls again," Sasha said with a sigh.

"Then avoid the bathroom between one-thirty and two-thirty," Jade advised. "That's their dis-Burdine fest."

"I thought the Tweevils worshipped the great Queen of Pink," Sasha said.

"Hardly," Jade replied. "Those back-stabbers worship a good dis even more."

"Hmmm," Yasmin said thoughtfully. "That's very interesting."

Cloe could tell Yasmin had come up with something.

"What are you thinking, Pretty Princess?" she asked.

"Just that I think it's time we teach the Tweevils a lesson," Yasmin responded, a mischievous twinkle in her eye.

Chapter Four

"Ugh!" Kaycee said to Kirstee. "I think I have a zit on my nose. There! I popped it!"

She and Kirstee were standing in front of the mirror in the bathroom. Kirstee was fixing her hair, and Kaycee was examining her face under the not-so-flattering fluorescent lights.

"Quit it!" Kirstee told her sister, smacking her on the arm. "You're, like, grossing me out."

"My nose job isn't as bad as Burdine's, is it?" Kaycee asked as she examined her profile in the mirror.

"Are you kidding?" Kirstee replied. "Hers is all pointy and bony, like an icky bird beak."

Kaycee cackled at her sister's nickname. "Do you think Bird Face has had other work done?"

"Totally," Kirstee said knowingly. "I'll bet she's had lipo and a face-lift, and her lips are full of silicone. That's why they look like big, fat rotting sausages."

"How old do you think she is?" Kaycee asked.

"She's so ancient," Kirstee said, flipping her hair over her shoulder. "She has to be *at least* thirty."

Jade stifled a giggle from inside one of the stalls. She leaned over and flushed the toilet. Then she put on her best Burdine accent. "Mother of pink!" she said, loud enough for Kirstee and Kaycee to hear.

Kaycee and Kirstee froze. They peered into the mirror to check the stalls behind them. Kirstee nudged Kaycee, pointing to a pair of pink pumps under the third stall. Kaycee's eyes widened, and the two girls dashed for the bathroom door.

As soon as they had left, Cloe, Yasmin, and Sasha popped out over the tops of the other three stalls.

"Way to go, girl!" Sasha told Jade as they all emerged from their stalls.

"You totally evened the score," Cloe said as Jade gave each of her friends a high five.

Kirstee and Kaycee tried to sneak back into the office, but Burdine caught them skulking by.

"Well?!" Burdine demanded. She was sitting at her desk pulling tiny pink curlers out of Royale's hair.

"We are, like, so sorry," Kirstee said apologetically. "We didn't mean any of those things we said."

"We don't really think your lips look like big, fat rotting sausages," Kaycee added.

Royale looked at Burdine's lips, then at Kaycee, and then back at Burdine, who stood up angrily.

"Or that you have a pointy, bony, icky bird-beak nose," Kirstee said.

"And that you're thirty . . ." Kirstee put in.

Burdine's face turned bright red. "Thirty?!" she shrieked. "You think I'm thirty?!"

She moved toward the girls, picking up a small picture frame from her desk.

Royale growled menacingly, and Kirstee and Kaycee started stepping backward gingerly.

"My nose!" Kaycee cowered, covered her face with her hands. "Please don't hurt my nose!"

The Tweevils ducked for cover as the picture frame crashed into the wall behind them. As Kirstee crouched down, she noticed Burdine's pink and white shoes. She groaned, realizing that the shoes in the bathroom had been solid pink.

"Uh-oh," she said, nudging Kaycee and pointing to the shoes.

"Whoops!" Kaycee cried as she dodged a pad of Post-Its.

"Run for it!" Kirstee yelled as they dashed out of the office.

Back at the newly remodeled magazine headquarters, the girls got down to work. Cloe sat at the computer, typing furiously. She was working on her first "Dear Cloe" advice column. Just the other day, one of the girls in her math class had asked Cloe for advice on what she should wear on her first date with a guy who had been her best friend for years. Cloe thought that would be a great first question for her column, and she had the perfect answer! A pretty sparkly sweater, low-ridin' jeans, and some funky boots would be just right.

Meanwhile, Yasmin was checking out the digital camera to make sure it was working properly. She kept snapping shots of her friends to test it out.

"Yasmin, cut it out!" Jade said as she flipped through the Hot Models portfolio book. "I'm so not even posing for those pictures you keep snapping."

"Chill, Kool Kat," Yasmin said. "I'm just testing the camera. No one will see these photos, I promise."

"You can snap shots of me, Pretty Princess," Sasha said. She was busy practicing some new dance moves while she rocked out to some hot new hip-hop grooves. She was planning a story for the magazine that reviewed the latest hip-hop CD *and* showcased a few smokin' new moves.

"Thanks, Bunny Boo," Yasmin said. Then she thought of something that was even more important than the digital camera. "Hey, any idea what we're gonna call our fab new magazine?" she asked her friends.

"How about . . . *Sasha*?" Sasha teased as she did a funky twist.

"Sasha!" Yasmin sighed, rolling her eyes. Cloe and Jade shot Sasha looks, too.

"You guys!" Sasha said. "I was only playin' with you."

"Seriously, though, that's a good question, Yas," Cloe said thoughtfully. "We need something stylin'."

"Yeah," said Sasha. "Something with attitude."

"But not *too* much attitude," Jade added, thinking of Kaycee and Kirstee. "Hey! I've got it!"

"What is it, Kool Kat?" Cloe asked.

"Brats!" Jade shouted enthusiastically.

"Are you kidding?" Cloe asked, incredulous. "That's what the Tweevils call us!"

"I know," Jade said as she picked up a fat black marker and wrote B-R-A-T-S in large letters on a dry-erase board.

So, we make it our own?" Yasmin asked.

"Exactly!" Jade said.

"We've got to give it some attitude, though," Sasha mused, leaning over to wipe off the S. She scribbled a big *Z* in its place.

"Hmmm . . ." Yasmin considered the name. "Maybe there's a little *too* much attitude?"

"Hold on," Cloe said, picking up the marker and drawing an angelic halo over the *R* and the *A*.

"*Bratz*!" the four girls exclaimed together.

"Love it!" Yasmin said.

"Feel it!" said Sasha.

"Totally smokin'," Jade said.

"Awesome," Cloe said as she turned back to the computer. "Now let's think about our first major scoop."

"Say no more," responded Jade. "I just happen to have saved a bunch of invitations that Burdine told me to toss!"

She reached for her bag and turned it upside down over the table. A handful of brightly colored invitations tumbled out of the bag. Jade picked up a hot pink envelope and slid the invite out. She scanned it quickly and suddenly jumped out of her chair, waving the invite over her head.

"You are not going to believe this," she told her friends. "Superstylin' fashion reporter Jade scoops the biggest scoop of all scoops *ever*."

The other girls gathered around Jade and tried to read over her shoulder.

Sasha squealed. "Those are invitations to the exclusive opening of Pinz, the most hap new punk rock club!"

"No way!" Cloe said.

"*And* there are tickets to the Save the Universe Benefit Concert!" Jade continued reading.

"Get OUT!" Yasmin shouted.

"Off the hook!" Sasha said, swiveling her hips and doing a little dance move.

"Every rock star in the world is going to be there," Jade explained. "And this invitation is for an all-expenses-paid trip for six magazine staff members, including accommodations in a five-star luxury hotel suite. And we've got first-class plane tickets—to London!"

The girls squealed in delight.

Sasha grabbed the invitation and kissed it.

"We rock!" she shouted.

"We're hot!" added Jade.

"We're the girls with a passion for fashion," Cloe said. "And we're going to London!"

The girls high-fived. Starting their own magazine was turning out to be a *very* good idea.

Chapter Five

Sasha plopped into her enormous first-class seat, kicked up her feet, and took a sip of her freshly squeezed orange juice. "Now, this is living!" she said with a sigh as she slipped on her headphones and fastened her seatbelt.

Yasmin sat down next to her and did a few mini yoga poses. "These seats are so enormous, there's room for me to practice my yoga!" she squealed with delight.

Behind them, Cloe and Cameron chatted across the aisle.

"This trip is going to be so awesome, Cameron," Cloe gushed.

"Totally," Cameron replied. "I'm really glad you girls asked Dylan and me to tag along. Maybe we can go see Big Ben together."

"Sure, if we have time," Cloe said with a smile.

A tall guy stopped in front of Cloe. He looked down

at his ticket, a puzzled expression on his face.

"Excuse me," he said to Cloe with a British accent. "I do believe you're in my seat."

Cloe took out her ticket and looked at the seat number. She realized he was right. "Oops! Sorry, my mistake," she said sweetly, sliding over into the next seat. She couldn't believe her luck! Not only was she flying to London with her three best friends to cover the hottest club opening for their new fashion mag, but she was also sitting next to a total hottie. *And* he had a British accent! *It can't get any better than this*, Cloe thought to herself.

"Allow me to introduce myself," he said to Cloe as he took his seat and held out his hand to her. "I am Nigel Forrester, the ninth Duke of Lessex."

"And I'm Cloe, but my friends call me Angel," she replied, grasping his hand. "It's nice to meet you!"

Her horoscope had said a handsome prince was going to carry her away on a horse, but a duke and a first-class plane ride to London wasn't too shabby. Cloe leaned back in her seat and closed her eyes, a smile on her lips.

Cameron, on the other hand, was totally bummed.

"Relax, dude!" Dylan told him. "It's only a ten-hour flight."

"Thanks, Dyl-man," Cameron said sarcastically as he turned to face his friend. "That makes me feel a

whole lot better."

He tapped Yasmin on the shoulder. "Hey, Yas," he said. "Tell me about this club again."

Yasmin untwisted her legs and sat up straight. "Pinz is supposed to be the most superstylin' punk club ever!"

Sasha removed her headphones. "And the benefit concert is going to be scorchin'! Every major rock star will be there."

"Poor Burdine," Jade said, shaking her head. "She's so clueless. She has no idea she threw out the party invitation of the year."

Back at Burdine's office, the Tweevils were busy lugging enormous pink suitcases out of Burdine's wardrobe closet. Kaycee pulled pink suits out of Burdine's closet and flung them into one suitcase, while Kirstee played tug-of-war with Royale over one of the suits.

"Give me that, you ugly little furball!" she shrieked, pulling. Then she heard a sickening rip. She quickly let go of the suit, giving Royale full possession.

"You mangy little rat," Kirstee scolded loudly. "Look what you've done to Mommy Burdine's suit!"

But Burdine was too busy stomping furiously around the office to notice.

"You idiot interns!" she yelled. "How dare you let me let Jade throw out the invitation of the year?"

"But we weren't even in the office when it happened!" Kaycee whined in protest.

"Yeah!" Kirstee added lamely.

"Spare me your excuses!" Burdine shouted. "*Your Thing* will not be out-scooped by the amateur *Bratz Magazine* or I'll have you two hung upside down by your shoe straps! Now how come my suitcases aren't packed already? Hurry up! Chop, chop!"

Jade peered out the window at the dark sky. She saw a few glittering lights on the ground below.

"Hey, guys!" she exclaimed. "I think we're almost there!"

Just at that moment, the flight attendant announced that they were beginning their descent to Heathrow International Airport.

"England, here we come!" Sasha said excitedly.

Cloe looked out the window on her side of the plane. "Look! I can see Big Ben!"

Cameron smiled at the idea of wandering around Big Ben with Cloe, hand in hand. But then he heard Nigel's British accent and his smile disappeared.

"If I may be so bold," Nigel said to Cloe, "it would be

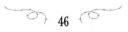

my honor to show you Big Ben tomorrow."

Cloe looked at Nigel and smiled.

"Really?" she asked.

"But of course," Nigel replied smoothly.

Once they got off the plane, the girls found a limo waiting to take them to the Q Hotel.

"The invitation says we'll be staying in the Q's superstylin' supreme suite," Jade said.

"I feel like a movie star!" Cloe gushed. "First-class plane tickets, a limo, and a deluxe suite. Can it get any better than this?"

The limo sped through London. Yasmin had her face glued to the window as they passed shop after shop. Each window display was funkier than the next.

"Hey, girls," Yasmin said. "What time do we have to be at the hotel?"

"Well, I scheduled an editorial meeting for us later this afternoon," Sasha said. Cloe, Yasmin, and Jade shot her withering looks.

"I mean, if you guys want to go over some things," Sasha continued sheepishly. "But I don't think we need to be there before then."

"Great," Yasmin said. "'Cuz I know we could all stretch our legs out a little bit after that flight. And you

know what that means . . ."

"SHOPPING!" they shouted together.

Cameron and Dylan looked at each other.

"Sounds good to me," Cameron shrugged.

Five minutes later, they piled out of the limo in front of a hip store with an enormous British flag hanging in the window.

"This looks like a good place to start," Sasha said. "Come on, girls. Let's hit it!"

A few hours later, Jade, Sasha, Cloe, Yasmin, Cameron, and Dylan arrived at their hotel laden down with luggage and about twenty enormous shopping bags.

Cloe plopped down onto the gigantic bed.

"Whew!" she exclaimed. "Having a passion for fashion can be really exhausting!"

"Tell me about it," Jade agreed. "And now we're having an editorial meeting to discuss our plans for tomorrow."

"That's right," Sasha piped up, pulling out her notebook. "Let's go over our assignments."

The others nodded and pulled out their own notebooks.

"Yasmin and I will scope out the ten best places to find the cutest guys," Cloe said.

"Cameron and Dylan are going to cover sports and

entertainment," Yasmin added.

"And Jade and I will scoop the London fashion scene," Sasha told the group. "I've already mapped out all the superstylin' places I want to check out."

"Sasha," Jade sighed. "You mean where *we* want to go."

She looked over Sasha's list. "Hey! Notting Hill isn't on here!"

"Chill, Kool Kat," Sasha assured her. "We'll get to it."

"Fine," Jade snapped, irritated. Sasha could be bossy sometimes, but it wasn't like her to totally dismiss Jade's ideas.

"Meeting adjourned!" Sasha announced. "Now it's time for a little beauty rest."

Meanwhile, somewhere over the ocean, Burdine, Royale, and the Tweevils were still nowhere near London. Burdine was reclining in her first-class seat, her aromatherapy face mask firmly in place, when Royale suddenly noticed a bulldog sitting across the aisle next to a man in dark black shades and a baseball cap. Royale jumped out of his seat and dashed across the aisle, barking and nipping at the other dog.

"Mother of pink!" Burdine exclaimed. "Would you

please control your fat mutt?"

"Excuse me?" the man responded archly in a British accent. "But *your* pathetic, hairy rat is attacking *my* Ozzy."

At the sound of his name, Ozzy's ears perked straight up, and he growled at Burdine. Burdine growled back.

"Stuff it, tubbo," Burdine barked.

"Come on, Ozzy," the man said, coaxing him back into his seat. "Let's leave the nasty woman and her mongrel alone."

Ozzy obediently jumped into his owner's lap.

"You haven't seen the last of me," Burdine said menacingly, wagging her finger at the man and Ozzy.

The next second, the plane hit a pocket of turbulence, and Burdine's water glass flew up, splashing water down the front of her freshly pressed pink suit.

"Mother of pink!" she cried.

The man stifled a laugh as her turned back to his book.

The next morning, the girls rose bright and early to get a jump on the day's assignments.

"Come on, Pretty Princess," Cloe said to Yasmin.

"Let's hit the London Eye. It's supposed to be London's hottest hangout!"

"I am so there," Yasmin answered.

Just as they started out the door, Cloe's cell rang.

"That must be my mother, *again*," she said, picking up the phone. "Mom, I am *not* wearing those rubber boots you snuck in my suit—oh, Nigel! Hi!"

Yasmin, Jade, and Sasha gathered around Cloe. She covered the phone with her hand.

"Oh my gosh, it's him!" she whispered.

"Talk, girl!" Sasha ordered.

Cloe turned back to the phone. "Of course I remember you! Right now? Sure, I'm not doing anything. See you in ten."

She hung up the phone and turned back to her friends, frantic.

"Oh, no!" she panicked. "I've got a date with Nigel and only five minutes to accessorize!"

"Um, Angel?" Yasmin said. "The London Eye?"

"We'll check it out later, 'kay?" Cloe said hurriedly.

"Yeah, sure," Yasmin said, smiling at Cloe's excitement.

"Thanks, Yas!" Cloe gushed. "You rock!"

And with that, she rushed out the door.

Chapter Six

Cloe gazed into Nigel's eyes across the table. They had spent the entire day together sightseeing around London, and now they were at a nice restaurant enjoying a romantic dinner for two.

"Thanks for the corsage, Nigel," Cloe said as she pinned the red rose onto her sweater. "It's really beautiful."

"Not nearly as beautiful as you, my Pretty Princess," Nigel flirted.

Cloe's smiled, embarrassed. Pretty Princess was Yasmin's nickname, and while Cloe was glad Nigel liked her, it felt weird to hear him using her friend's name.

"You know," Nigel went on. "I don't believe I've ever felt this way about a girl before."

Cloe laughed nervously. "Nigel, we just met."

"You don't believe in love at first sight?" he responded.

Cloe smiled shyly as the band began to play a waltz. Nigel stood and offered Cloe his hand. "Ah! A waltz!" he said. "Shall we dance?"

Cloe took Nigel's hand and followed him onto the dance floor. Cloe was on cloud nine as Nigel spun her around on the dance floor. First her own advice column, then a free trip to London, and now this? She felt like the luckiest girl on the planet. Could this truly be for real? Had Cloe actually found the Prince Charming her horoscope had mentioned?

After five or six dances and dessert, it was time to go. Nigel and Cloe said good night under a sparkling chandelier in the hotel lobby.

"I had an awesome time, Nigel," Cloe said. "Thank you."

"The pleasure was mine," he responded with a smile as he took her hand in his own. "May I see you again tomorrow?"

Cloe felt her cheeks flush as she looked into Nigel's eyes. "Sure, that would be great."

Nigel lifted her hand to his lips and kissed it softly.

"Until then, good-bye," he said as he turned to leave.

Cloe drifted up to the suite. She still couldn't believe how amazing her date with Nigel had been. When she entered the suite, she found Yasmin, Sasha, and Jade poring over a map of the London Underground while Cameron and Dylan were busy channel surfing.

"Man!" Dylan exclaimed as he flipped through the handful of stations that got reception in the hotel room. "How do the Brits channel surf with only five channels?!"

Yasmin heard the doorknob turn, and she looked up from the map to see Cloe enter the suite. "Cloe! How was your date with Prince Charming?" she asked.

"Prince Charming?!" Cameron scowled under his breath.

"Tell us everything!" Jade gushed as she, Sasha, and Yasmin surrounded Cloe.

"Yeah, spill it!" urged Sasha.

"It was amazing!" Cloe gushed. "We went to a really romantic restaurant, had a perfect dinner, and then we waltzed!"

"Uh, what's a waltz?" asked Dylan.

"It's what old people do," Cameron said drily. He didn't look pleased.

Yasmin turned to Cloe. "Well, I'm glad you had a good time, Angel. We're still on for the Eye tomorrow, right?"

"Maybe later in the day," Cloe responded. "Nigel invited me to his family's castle. And, well, when he called me his Pretty Princess, I just couldn't say no."

"Pretty Princess?" Yasmin said, sounding hurt. "That's *my* nickname." She exchanged a sympathetic look with Sasha and Jade.

Cloe glanced away, feeling a little guilty about using Yasmin's nickname. But she just couldn't say no to Nigel . . . he was way too cute.

I'll explain the whole thing to Nigel tomorrow, Cloe thought to herself. *And I'll make it up to Yasmin then, too.*

The next day, Cloe and Nigel pulled up in front of his family's castle in Nigel's convertible. At Nigel's voice command, the gates opened, and he and Cloe drove up a long drive to the front door. Cloe's jaw dropped as she took in the five turrets and the enormous double doors that swung open in front of them.

"Wow, Nigel," Cloe gushed. "This is so beautiful."

Nigel didn't seem to hear her. "Come, Pretty Princess," he said. "We're running late for the croquet match."

Once they got out on the lawn, Nigel handed Cloe a mallet and tried to show her how to hold it, but she couldn't quite get the hang of it. Skateboarding was way easier than this, and she kept getting distracted by the fantastic, sweeping views of the countryside around them.

"Nigel, your place is so awesome," Cloe said in a dreamy voice.

"Yes, it has its charms," he replied patiently. "Come now, darling, keep your eye on the ball."

Cloe swung the mallet and hit the ball through one of the wire hoops.

"Yes!" she cried, jumping up and down.

"Bravo!" Nigel shouted with encouragement. "I think you're getting the hang of it."

"That's because you rock as a teacher," Cloe said, batting her eyelashes.

"Compliment noted and accepted," replied Nigel.

Cloe's cell phone rang. She stepped off the course and flipped her phone open.

"Oh, hi, Yasmin," she said into the phone. "What's up?"

"What's up?" Yasmin snapped, exasperated. "It's almost four o'clock! You were supposed to be here at three to check out the London Eye with me."

"Oh, Yas!" Cloe cried. "I am so sorry! I completely spaced. Um, I can probably make it in an hour or so."

"Forget it," Yasmin said with a sigh. "I'll do the story myself. Later."

Yasmin hung up her phone and slipped it back into

her bag. She felt a few drops of water on her head and she realized it had started to rain. Just as she reached into her bag for her umbrella, she looked down to find an adorable bulldog looking up at her, his paw outstretched.

"Hi, cutie," Yasmin said, scooping him up. "Where'd you come from? Are you lost?" She patted his head and flipped his dog tag over. It simply read: OZZY.

"Aww," Yasmin cooed. "Hi there, Ozzy!"

Ozzy licked her face with a sweet slurp.

"You're a sweetie, aren't you?" Yasmin said as Ozzy burrowed deeper into her arms, resting his head on her shoulder. He whimpered in response.

"I know just how you feel," Yasmin comforted him. "I've lost my best friend, too. C'mon, sweetie. Let's go before we get soaked."

She tucked him into her bag and covered them both with her umbrella as she headed into The Eye by herself.

Across town, Sasha was busy standing under an awning snapping candid shots of pedestrians in hip-hop shots. Jade stood nearby, scowling.

"C'mon, Bunny Boo," she complained. "Can I *please* have some camera time?"

Sasha turned the camera and pressed a few buttons. "Uh-oh," she said. "No more memory."

"But I haven't even taken *one* shot!" Jade protested.

"You will!" Sasha promised. "Now, let's jam. I've planned this whole day and I don't want to miss our magazine deadline."

"You planned the whole day without consulting me?" Jade shouted, furious. "*Again?*!"

"Jade, would you chill already?" Sasha asked. "I know what I'm doing."

"Right," Jade scoffed.

The girls headed back to the hotel without speaking to each other.

Back at the suite, Yasmin was typing her article on the computer with Ozzy sitting in her lap when Sasha and Jade came in.

"Guys, I'm so glad you're here!" Yasmin exclaimed. "Cloe's totally bailed on me, but I found the cutest little—"

Sasha stormed into her room and slammed the door. Jade strode across the room in the opposite direction, slamming her door shut, as well.

"—dog," Yasmin trailed off dejectedly. What was going on with her friends? First Cloe ditched her for snooty Nigel, and now Sasha and Jade weren't talking to her, either. This trip to London was definitely not turning out the way she had expected.

Elsewhere in the hotel, Kaycee and Kirstee were busy unpacking and ironing Burdine's suitcases full of pink suits. The room they were sharing with Burdine was in the basement and only slightly bigger than the queen-sized bed in it.

"Can you believe those fashion-challenged Bratz named a magazine after themselves?" Kirstee scowled.

"Yeah!" Kaycee agreed. "They are, like, so totally self-absorbed."

"Those brazen Bratz will pay for this!" Burdine shrieked. "*All* of this! Stealing our room, daring to start a rival magazine, *and* having the audacity to try to out-scoop us!"

Burdine looked at the twins, who were busy ironing her skirts.

"Pay attention to me when I'm ranting!" she barked at them. Royale growled in agreement.

The Tweevils stopped ironing, leaving the irons flat on the skirts. Smoke billowed up on either side of each iron, but they focused on Burdine.

"I will get those girls and put their rotten little magazine out of business even if it kills you!" Burdine

screamed. "They cannot, and will not, succeed! Do you understand? And what is that horrible burning smell?"

Kirstee and Kaycee looked down at the skirts they were ironing, which were practically on fire.

"Mother of pink!" Burdine shouted.

Back in the Bratz suite, Cloe and Nigel had returned from their croquet outing. Sasha sat at the computer downloading her pictures, Yasmin was busy feeding Ozzy doggy treats, and Jade sat on the couch, furiously turning the pages of a magazine without even looking at them. She was still really upset with Sasha for hogging the camera the previous day.

Cloe walked across the room to the hotel phone and picked up the receiver.

"I am going to order a pot of tea," she said in a fake British accent. "Anyone care to join me?"

"Cloe, you hate tea," Sasha reminded her. "And what's with your voice?"

Cloe switched back to her regular voice, covering the mouthpiece of the phone. "Actually, I've grown quite fond of—" She lifted her hand from the mouthpiece. "One pot of tea, please," she said into the phone, using the fake accent again.

"As I was saying earlier, croquet requires intense

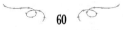

concentration," Nigel said, totally interjecting himself into the girls' conversation. "Isn't that right, Pretty Princess?"

"I don't know," Yasmin answered. "I've never played."

"Huh?" Nigel asked, confused.

"Nigel," Cloe said in her British accent. "Yasmin's nickname is also Pretty Princess."

Nigel turned to Yasmin. "Really?!" he asked, incredulous. "I'd say you're more of a Peaches."

"Peaches?!" Yasmin protested. She didn't like the way that sounded one bit.

Nigel didn't respond. Instead he got up, put his jacket on, and headed for the door.

"I'll see you tomorrow, Pretty Princess," he said to Cloe. "Cheerio, Peaches."

"Cheerio!" Yasmin chirped back, annoyed.

"See you tomorrow, Nigel," Cloe said as she walked him to the door. Once he had gone, she turned back to her friends.

"Guys, isn't he awesome?" she gushed, a dreamy look on her face.

"Totally awesome," Yasmin replied sarcastically.

Suddenly Jade stood up, tossing her magazine aside. She walked across the room and grabbed the camera from Sasha angrily. "I'm going out to take some of *my own*

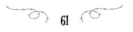

photos," she said as she headed for the door. "Later."

"Yo, Kool Kat," Sasha said defensively. "Are you upset with me? Because if you've got something to say to me, spill it."

"Fine!" Jade replied. "You are the biggest, bossiest control freak I've ever met. You're even worse than Burdine!"

"Whoa!" Yasmin said. "That is *harsh*."

"C'mon, guys," Cloe stepped in. "Chill out."

Sasha whipped around to face Cloe. "Puh-lease! Like you even know what's going on," she snapped. "You haven't even been around."

"No kidding," Jade added. "Yasmin's had to cover every hot spot by herself."

Cloe turned to Yasmin. "But Yasmin, you don't mind, do you?"

"Yes, I do," Yasmin said softly. "I mean, next thing you know, you'll be telling us you can't make it to the opening of Pinz!"

Cloe gasped. "Oh my gosh! I totally spaced! Nigel's brother is giving a dinner party tomorrow and I promised I'd go."

"Cloe," Sasha chided her friend. "Getting that scoop for our magazine is the reason we're even *in* London!"

Jade narrowed her eyes a bit and turned to Cloe. "Or have you forgotten that we're starting our own magazine?" she added.

Just at that moment, there was a knock at the door. Cameron and Dylan entered the room to find the four girls glaring at one another.

"Bad news, guys," Cameron said.

"Burdine and the Tweevils are here," Dylan added.

The girls didn't respond. Cameron and Dylan knew something was up. When these four girls were together in a room, there was *never* silence.

"Uh, what is going on?" Cameron asked.

The girls stormed out of the suite one after the other.

Dylan looked at Cameron and shrugged. "Girl stuff."

Chapter Seven

Later that evening, the girls were all back in the suite, though they still weren't talking to one another. Sasha was back at the computer working on her fashion layout. After their big fight, Jade had gone out to snap some of her own fashion shots, which she'd downloaded onto the computer. Sasha clicked the mouse to open the folder.

"Wow!" Sasha gasped as she saw the amazing photos. "Now, *these* are stylin'!"

There was a knock at the door. Cloe dashed out of her room to answer it. "Nigel, hi! You remember Sasha."

"Hey," Sasha said, looking up from the computer.

Nigel ignored her, picking up the newspaper instead.

"Whatever," Sasha muttered under her breath. She couldn't believe Cloe would be with someone who was so totally *not* into her friends!

"Nigel, my friends are covering the opening of this happenin' new punk rock club for our magazine," Cloe said. "We could go after the dinner party."

Nigel glanced at his watch distractedly. "We'll discuss it later. Now hurry up and get dressed. We don't want to be late. Chop, chop!"

Sasha looked up from the computer again.

"Um, I am dressed," Cloe replied.

"Dressed?" Nigel scoffed. "Darling, you can't be serious! Surely you must have something that's a little more elegant and understated. You know, like what those two lovely girls eavesdropping outside your door are wearing."

"What?!" Sasha shrieked, jumping up and throwing open the door to the suite. Kaycee and Kirstee stumbled into the room.

"Oh, hi," Kirstee said sweetly. "We were just passing by."

"And you got glued to our door?" Sasha asked, raising her eyebrows.

Kaycee stood up and dusted herself off. "It's really him! Nigel Forrester! The Duke of Lessex!"

"Get lost!" Kirstee shoved Kaycee aside. "I saw him first!"

Nigel was clearly flattered at the recognition. He

cleared his throat. "Correction," he stated. "I'm Nigel Forrester, the *ninth* Duke of Lessex."

Sasha rolled her eyes, while Cloe looked annoyed.

"I *so* like your tie," Kirstee gushed.

"And I *so* love your taste," Nigel said, imitating Kirstee's tone.

Sasha began ushering the Tweevils out the door. "Break it up, sisters!" she said. "Mutual admiration time is over!" She shoved them out and slammed the door.

Nigel turned to Sasha, appalled. "Excuse me," he said haughtily. "I hardly think such rude behavior was called for, especially since those girls were rather attractive."

"Nigel!" Cloe said, hurt.

He turned back to Cloe. "But not as attractive as you, Pretty Princess! Now, move along. We really must be going."

Cloe grabbed her jacket and followed Nigel out the door. "Later, Sasha."

Jade came out of her bedroom and pulled off her headphones.

"What's going on out here?" Jade asked. "I thought I heard the Tweevils."

"Don't ask," Sasha sighed. "You definitely do not want to know. But I've been working on our photo layout, and I want your opinion. Would you take a look?"

"*Our* layout?" Jade asked, surprised. She

walked over to the computer and looked over Sasha's shoulder. "Bunny Boo! You used all of my pictures!"

"Yours were way better," Sasha said. "You know you have a scorchin' sense of fashion."

"Thanks, Sasha." Jade smiled at her friend.

"Look, I'm sorry about everything," Sasha told Jade. "You know how I can get."

"That's okay," Jade replied, giving Sasha a big hug. "Apology accepted."

Yasmin, Dylan, and Cameron entered the room to find Jade and Sasha hugging. "Best friends again?" Yasmin asked with a smile.

"Forever!" Jade and Sasha exclaimed together.

Dylan and Cameron looked at each other. Cameron raised his eyebrows and shrugged.

"Did I miss something?" Dylan asked.

"No idea," Cameron said, shaking his head.

"C'mon!" Sasha cried. "We've gotta look totally punkalicious for the opening of Pinz."

"Are you thinking what I'm thinking?" Yasmin asked.

"Time to hit the shops for some totally hot new outfits!" Sasha exclaimed.

With that, Sasha, Yasmin, Jade, Cameron, and Dylan headed out the door.

Cloe stood on the veranda of Nigel's family's castle, looking out at the dark English countryside around her. During the day the view had been sweeping and beautiful, but in the dark, the void in front of her just made her feel even lonelier than she already was.

"There you are," Nigel said as he came up behind her. "I've been looking all over for you. In case you've forgotten, there's a party inside."

"Sorry, Nigel," Cloe sighed. "I was just taking five. You know, the Pinz opening starts at—"

"Oh, *really*, Cloe," Nigel said, exasperated. "I wouldn't be caught dead at some tacky punk rock club. I mean, it's so low class."

Cloe was really offended by Nigel's remarks. "I don't think so," she argued. "Punk clubs rule. Besides, I miss hanging out with my friends."

"Those misfits?" Nigel scoffed. "Come now, my Pretty Princess. Those girls are *so* uncouth!"

Cloe turned to him, furious. There was no way she was going to let him talk about her best friends like that.

"They are so *not* uncouth!" she shouted at him. "You just don't understand them, you royal jerk!"

Nigel took a step back. "And you, my Pretty Princess,

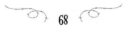

are way out of line," he said haughtily.

"Stop calling me Pretty Princess," Cloe protested. "My friends call me Angel."

Suddenly, Kirstee burst out onto the balcony.

"Dukey!" Kirstee shouted. "There you are!"

She leaned out over the railing to take in the view. "This balcony is, like, so beautiful!"

Nigel swung around to face Kirstee, turning his back on Cloe. "Not nearly as beautiful as you, my Pretty Princess," he said.

Kirstee batted her eyelashes at Nigel. Cloe couldn't believe what she was hearing. She rolled her eyes as Kirstee and Nigel bantered back and forth.

"You know, I've never felt this way about a girl before," Nigel said smoothly.

Kirstee giggled with delight. "But Dukey, we just met!" she squealed.

"Don't you believe in love at first sight, Kirstee?" Cloe asked sarcastically. Then she turned and walked out. She had better places to be than this royal wreck of a party.

Once Cloe got outside the castle, though, her demeanor broke. She thought about how much she'd neglected her friends the past few days, and how much fun she had missed out on. As the tears started to flow, she looked at her watch and realized she was going to be late for the Pinz opening. She broke out into a run. As she ran, she slipped out of one of her shoes, but she was too distraught to notice.

Then out of nowhere, Cameron pulled up on his motorcycle. "Hi," he said.

"Cameron, hi!" Cloe said, wiping her tears. "What are you doing here?"

"Just going for a ride," Cameron replied. Then he reached into a compartment on his motorcycle and pulled out a sparkling silver platform shoe.

"My shoe!" Cloe cried. "You found it!"

Cameron leaned down and slipped the shoe back onto Cloe's foot. Then he straightened up and handed her a helmet.

"Hold on, Angel," Cameron told her as she climbed onto the motorcycle behind him. Cloe grasped Cameron tightly and leaned her head against his back. As they rode through the streets of London, she looked up to see a full moon rising over Big Ben.

Chapter Eight

Yasmin, Sasha, Jade, and Dylan were busy getting ready for the opening. Jade was putting her hair up in funky half-pigtails, and Yasmin was putting the finishing touches on her make-up. Sasha was totally ready to go, and Dylan was busy checking his camera.

"Remember, Dylan, you have to take pictures of guys as well as girls," she reminded him. "Our readers will want to see both."

"Check it, Bunny Boo," Dylan responded.

There was the sound of a key in the door to the suite, and the door swung open to reveal Cameron and Cloe.

"Hi, guys," Cloe said shyly.

"Cloe!" Yasmin shouted, elated.

Cloe took a deep breath. "Guys, I've had an over-the-top emotional breakthrough," she declared. "These past few days I haven't been true to myself or to any of you. I am so sorry. I can totally understand if you never want to talk to me again."

She looked down at her feet.

"Girls, I think our resident drama mama is back," Sasha joked.

Cloe looked up at her friends and broke out into a smile. She took in her friends' punkalicious outfits and hairdos. "Wow!" she said. "You guys look so pretty in punk."

"Thanks," Jade replied. "We're feelin' ready for the Pinz opening tonight."

"There's one for you too, Angel," Yasmin added, holding up a totally punky outfit.

"I can't believe it!" Cloe gasped. "You got that for me?!"

"Yeah," Yasmin responded. "Just in case you could make it."

"You know, Yasmin, there really is only one Pretty Princess," Cloe reminded her friend.

"And there's only one Angel," Yasmin responded.

"Best friends?" Cloe asked.

"Forever!" Yasmin agreed as she reached out to give Cloe a huge hug.

The group arrived at the club just as the party was getting underway. Yasmin hadn't wanted to leave Ozzy

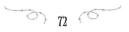

alone in the hotel room, so she had brought him along, too. An enormous bouncer dressed entirely in black and wearing black sunglasses stopped them at the front door of Pinz. Cloe turned on the charm.

"Hi," she said sweetly. "There are six of us with *Bratz*—I mean, *Your Thing* magazine."

The bouncer scanned his list quickly. "Got any ID?" he asked.

"Uh-oh," Yasmin whispered to Sasha. "Don't look now, but the Tweevils are heading this way!"

Sure enough, it was Burdine, Royale, Kirstee, and Kaycee.

Burdine pushed past Dylan, Cameron, and the girls and pointed her finger in the bouncer's face. "I demand you have these girls arrested for impersonation!"

"And for pretending to be us!" Kaycee added.

"Yeah!" Kirstee agreed.

"Well, don't just stand there like a lump!" Burdine screamed at the bouncer. "Call the police! Now! Chop, chop!"

While Burdine was busy berating the bouncer, another passerby caught Yasmin's eye.

"Oh my gosh!" Yasmin whispered to her friends. "Major celebrity sighting! Everyone just act cool."

Cloe peered around Burdine to see who it was. "No way!" she gasped. "It's Byron Powell, the judge

73

from *America Rocks!*"

"That's my favorite show!" Sasha interjected.

Byron approached the girls and headed toward Yasmin. "You've found Ozzy," he told her, scooping Ozzy gently out of her arms. "I've been worried sick about him."

Yasmin's mouth dropped open. "*You're* his owner?" she asked, incredulous.

Byron nodded as Burdine's voice rose behind him. "Mother of pink!" she shrieked. "Arrest them! I want the whole lot of them handcuffed!"

"Oh, no," Byron said, rolling his eyes. "It's that absolutely horrific woman from the plane. Quick, girls! Follow me!"

Byron led the girls, Cameron, and Dylan right up to the bouncer.

"Hey, Edgar," Byron said to the man. "I brought a few friends."

Edgar lifted the red rope and Yasmin, Cloe, Sasha, Jade, Dylan, and Cameron followed Byron inside the club. Burdine and the Tweevils tried to sneak by as well, but Byron turned back to Edgar one last time.

"You do realize, Edgar, that those women are in gross violation of the dress code, don't you?" he asked innocently. "Pink doesn't mix with punk."

Edgar lowered the rope in front of Burdine and

crossed his arms firmly.

"Do you know who I am?" Burdine hissed. "You cannot do this! I am Burdine Maxwell, founder, president, editor-in-chief . . ."

Jade took one last look at Burdine and the Tweevils on the other side of the rope and turned to enter the club.

"This place is rockin'!" Cloe shouted over the loud punk music.

"Yeah," Jade agreed. "It's totally awesome!"

Sasha looked around the room, taking everything in. "There is only one word to describe this place," she told her friends. "Punkalicious!"

Byron leaned in to talk to Yasmin over the music. "So, how can I reward you for taking care of Ozzy?" he asked her.

"It was no problem," Yasmin said. "But since you offered, how about an interview for our new teen magazine?" She gestured to her friends.

Ozzy barked with approval.

"You know, I just signed a new band—Crash," Byron told Yasmin. "They're headlining the Save the Universe Benefit Concert tomorrow night."

"We've got tickets," Cloe interjected.

Byron turned to face the four girls. "Then how

would you like backstage passes *and* an interview with me after the show?"

"That would be fantastic," Yasmin said, turning to high-five her friends.

"Now let's hit the dance floor!" Sasha yelled.

Cameron turned to Cloe. "Shall we dance?"

She smiled as she took his hand and headed onto the dance floor.

Chapter Nine

"That party last night at Pinz was awesome!" Cloe gushed as she painted a coat of Fire Engine Red polish on Sasha's toes. She and the other girls were hanging out in their hotel suite, recapping the highlights of the previous evening.

Sasha lifted her foot up, wiggling her toes to check out the color. "I was so all over that dance floor!"

Yasmin looked up from the laptop she had been busy tapping. "And I met a mysterious man, just like my horoscope said. I still can't believe it was Byron Powell, the mean judge from *America Rocks!*"

"Your interview with him is gonna rock!" Sasha agreed.

"Well, my horoscope said a handsome prince would sweep me away on a horse," Cloe added. "It's more like I kissed a duke and he turned into a frog."

"Cheer up, Cloe," Sasha reassured her. "Tonight

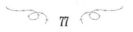

Bratz Magazine hits the Save the Universe Concert, and we've got front row seats to music-making history!"

"And thanks to Yasmin, we've also got backstage passes," Jade reminded them. "What do you girls say we check out Hyde Park before the concert?"

"Scorchin' idea!" Sasha said as Jade playfully tossed her a Frisbee.

As the girls got ready to head out, Cloe's cell phone rang.

"Not my mother *again*!" Cloe protested as she answered the phone. "Mom, I told you not to call. It's really expensive—oh, hi, Cameron. We were just leaving for Hyde Park. . . . Okay. See you there."

As they headed toward the door, Sasha turned to Yasmin. "Hey, Pretty Princess. The concert tickets are in a safe place, right? I don't want Burdine or those Tweevils to get their thievin' hands on them."

"Trust me, Bunny Boo," Yasmin reassured her. "I've got 'em stashed."

The girls headed out to the park to enjoy the London sunshine.

Twenty minutes later, the Tweevils were standing at the door to the girls' suite. They were dressed in identical black skirts and ridiculously frilly white blouses and bonnets.

"Hello?!" Kirstee squawked in a fake British accent. "Maid service! Anybody here?"

When there was no response, Kirstee and Kaycee managed to force the door open to enter the suite.

"Whoa!" Kaycee whispered. "This suite's, like, amazing! Look at all the neat stuff!"

She grabbed a bottle of lotion and squirted it on her hands. "Mmm . . . grapefruit-scented lotion."

Kirstee tried to grab the bottle out of Kirstee's hand. "Give it to me!" Kirstee screeched. "I saw it first!"

The lotion squirted out of the bottle and hit the mirror across the room.

"Gimme!" Kaycee yelled.

"No, you gimme!" Kirstee screamed.

"It's mine!" Kaycee and Kirstee shouted at the same time. They wrestled over the bottle of lotion for a minute or two until finally Kirstee wrenched it out of Kaycee's hand.

"Hey!" Kaycee pouted. "That's not fair."

Kirstee shrugged and then turned to rifle through some papers on the table. "We'd better find those tickets before Burdine kills us."

"Yeah," Kaycee concurred as she poked around in one of the suite's closets. "'Cause it'll be really hard to find them if we're dead."

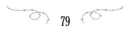 79

She pulled out a jacket. "Ooh! This jacket is, like, *soooo* cute."

"Ewww! Put that down! I'll bet it had cooties!" Kirstee shrieked as she grabbed the jacket and tossed it onto the closet floor. A flurry of tickets fell out of the pocket.

"Bingo!" Kirstee yelled. "Our lives are, like, *so* not over!"

"We're going to live!" Kaycee screamed as she hugged her sister. They jumped up and down together.

The beep of the key card interrupted their cheers.

"They're back!" Kirstee whispered. "Quick! Hide!"

She and Kaycee each slipped under a bed as Yasmin and Dylan entered. Yasmin had headed back from the park before the others to work on questions for her interview with Byron Powell, and Dylan had agreed to walk her back to the hotel.

"Mind if I hang out in here while room service cleans my suite?" Dylan asked.

"Only if you promise to be quiet," Yasmin said seriously. "I really have to concentrate on these questions."

"Okay, I promise I'll be quiet. But first, can you tell me what time the concert starts?" Dylan asked. "I want to make sure I have major mirror time to get ready."

"I'll check," Yasmin said as she headed to the closet. She reached into her pocket.

"Omigosh!" she shrieked. "The tickets are gone!"

Yasmin rushed around the suite, frantically searching the place. She and Dylan rifled through papers, opened and closed drawers, and looked through the pockets of all of the coats in the closet.

"I *know* I hid them in my jacket," Yasmin said. "Think! Think for me, Dylan!"

"I've got it!" Dylan said. "We'll wait for the others to get back and ask them what to do!"

"Dylan! Are you crazy?" Yasmin yelled. "Wait, don't answer that. No way am I telling them I lost the tickets. They're counting on this!"

Yasmin paced the suite, frantic.

"I can't believe this is happening! What am I going to do?" she flopped down stomach first on one the beds and covered her head with her hands. Then she rolled over and looked up at Dylan. Her eyes lit up as she thought of a plan. "I know! I'll find Byron. He'll get us in!"

Yasmin leaped up from the bed, grabbed her coat, and headed for the door. "Stay here and cover for me, okay? And don't tell anyone I lost the tickets!"

"No prob, Yas," Dylan assured her. "They'll have to

hang me by my toenails and force me to use generic shampoo."

"Cool," Yasmin replied. "I'll be back in a flash."

Chapter Ten

Yasmin practically ran the entire way to the theater where the Save the Universe Concert was going to be held. She tugged on the door to the theater, but it was locked.

What am I going to do? Yasmin thought to herself. *Our magazine so needs this scoop! I've just got to find Byron.*

She banged on the door with her fists and yelled as loud as she could.

"Byron! Open up!" she shouted desperately. "It's me, Yasmin. It's an emergency! Open up!"

Suddenly, the door swung open. It was the bouncer from the previous evening.

"Oh, thank you for opening the door!" Yasmin burst out, relieved. "I need to talk to Byron Powell. It's an emergency!"

The bouncer pointed to a sign next to the door. It read: BANDS ONLY. From the look on his face, Yasmin could tell that it wasn't even worth trying to argue with him or sweet-talk her way in. This guy wasn't going to budge.

She sighed. "My life is so over," she said softly to herself.

Meanwhile, back at the suite, Dylan was jumping up and down on one of the beds and practicing his air-guitar skills. While his back was to the door, the Tweevils managed to slip out without him noticing.

Dylan flopped down in a chair, exhausted from his air-guitar adventures. He heard voices outside the door of the suite, followed by the beep of a key card in the door. Jade, Sasha, and Cloe entered.

"Let's get to the concert early so we can hang with the bands before they go on," Sasha was telling her friends.

"Scorchin' idea, Sash," Jade responded.

"Hey, guys," Dylan greeted them.

"Hi, Dylan," Jade replied. "Where's Yasmin?"

Dylan fiddled with his imaginary guitar nervously. "Oh, she had to, um, go out."

"Really?" Sasha asked, curious. "Where to?"

Dylan searched for an answer. "Um, bowling," he blurted.

"Bowling?!" Cloe exclaimed. "Why would she go bowling?"

Sasha narrowed her eyes, suddenly suspicious. "You're hiding something, aren't you?" she asked.

"Me?" Dylan asked innocently. "No way . . . nothing to hide. So, um, what's new? Read any books lately?"

Jade, Cloe, and Sasha looked at one another. Dylan was *never* interested in discussing literature.

"Tickle fest!" Sasha yelled as she moved in on Dylan.

Cloe and Jade joined in.

"Tell us!" Cloe pleaded.

"Yeah, spill it!" Jade ordered.

Dylan fell back into the chair, laughing. "Okay, Okay!" he shouted, pushing the girls away from him. "I confess! Yasmin lost the concert tickets and is out trying to get new passes."

The girls' mouths dropped open in shock.

"Nooooo!" Cloe moaned. "Those tickets *cannot* be gone!"

"We've got to find them!" Sasha cried. "My music column depends on it."

"The whole *magazine* depends on it!" Jade added.

Sasha began pacing the room, her fists clenched. "I told her to put those tickets in a safe place!"

"She said she did," Jade reminded her.

"Well, not safe enough!" Sasha snapped.

"Chill, Bunny Boo," Cloe soothed. "Yas is our friend. We've gotta hear her side of the story."

"You're right," Sasha replied. "Sorry I flipped out. Those tickets have got to be around here somewhere. We should probably take a look."

Yasmin entered the room just in time to hear Sasha's last few words. She could tell by the looks on her friends' faces that her secret was out. She spun around to face Dylan. "What?" she cried. "Dylan, how could you?!"

"Sorry, Yas," Dylan said, looking truly remorseful, "They tickled it out of me."

"Pretty Princess, why didn't you want to tell us?" Jade asked.

Yasmin sighed. "Oh, Kool Kat. I was afraid to let you guys and the magazine down."

Cloe shook her head. "Yasmin, tickets or no tickets, we still love you."

"Really?" Yasmin asked, her eyes glistening with tears.

"Of course!" Cloe said, giving Yasmin a huge hug. "Our friendship is way more important than some concert."

"You'd better believe it!" Sasha agreed.

"So where were you just now, anyway, Yas?" Jade asked.

"I went over the club to see if I could find Byron and asked him for some replacement tickets," Yasmin said with a sigh. "But he totally wasn't there. The only person I saw was that surly bouncer from the other night, and he said only bands were allowed in."

Suddenly something caught Sasha's eye. She bent down and plucked something off the floor.

"Hey, girls," Sasha said. "It looks like someone dropped an earring. Who wears pearls?"

"Not me," Cloe said.

"No way," Jade added. "Pearls are so what my mom wears."

"I know of a couple other people who wear pearl earrings . . ." Yasmin said as the answer dawned on her. "The Tweevils!"

Sasha gasped. "Pretty Princess, you didn't lose the tickets. Those seriously evil twins got in here and stole them."

Cloe flung herself down on the bed in despair. "Oh no! We'll never get the tickets back now! We might as well give up and go home and forget all our dreams and ambitions—"

Sasha put her hand over Cloe's mouth. "Chill, Angel," she said, shushing her.

"Well, no way am I going to let Burdine and the Tweevils destroy my dream again," Jade declared.

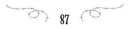

"You mean *our* dream, Kool Kat," Sasha asserted passionately. "Nothing is going to stop us from launching *Bratz Magazine*!"

Cloe struggled to free herself from Sasha's grip. "So, what are we going to do?" she pleaded.

Jade's eyes lit up. She had just thought of the perfect plan.

"Did you say they only let bands into the club?" Jade asked Yasmin.

Sasha turned to Jade with a conspiratorial look in her eye. "Are you thinking what I'm thinking?"

"I am *so* thinking what you're thinking," Jade said. "Let's become a rock band!"

Chapter Eleven

Sasha glanced at her metallic silver watch. "Look people, we've got less than four hours to put together a slammin' song and convince that bouncer that we're the real thing," she declared.

"Four hours?!" Cloe exclaimed. "We'll never make it."

"Chill, Angel," Sasha said confidently. "My horoscope said music's my thing and I *know* how to make it happen. Here's the plan. I'll work out the moves. Jade, you're in charge of wardrobe."

"On it!" Jade declared.

"Cloe and Yasmin, you two can write the song."

"Awesome!" Cloe said.

"And I'll be your roadie," Cameron chimed in, flashing Cloe a huge grin.

"I'll be your lead singer!" Dylan announced.

The girls gave him a look.

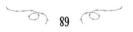

"Your backup singer?" he asked hopefully.

The girls gave him yet another look.

Sasha punched him playfully in the arm. "Actually, Dylan, you belong *behind* the camera," she told him. Then she grabbed the camera off of the table and tossed it his way.

"Paparazzi!" Dylan exclaimed. "That is hot! So, what are you going to call yourselves?"

"What else?" Sasha said, spinning around and throwing her arms out wide. "Sasha's Destiny!"

"Bunny Boo!" the other girls cried at once.

"Hey!" Sasha said quickly. "I was just kidding."

"Guys, this concert is about making a difference in the world," Jade reminded them.

"What about Sasha's Angelz?" Sasha asked innocently.

"Hold on," Yasmin said thoughtfully as she drummed her nails on the bedside table. "Angel . . . hmmmm . . . rock. What about Rock Angelz?"

"Yeah, I like that!" Cloe agreed. "Bratz Rock Angelz!"

"Love it!" Sasha shouted.

"Feel it!" Yasmin cried.

"Adore it!" Jade declared.

They were going to be the hottest new band to hit London.

Jade raced out the door and headed out to the shops to search for the perfect outfits. First, she tried a funky boutique with outfits in shiny metallic silvers and gold. The shirts had little wings on the sleeves and came with shiny moon boots. They were superstylin' but a little too far-out.

"No, thanks!" Jade called to the saleswoman as she jetted out the door to the next shop.

Jade whirled around the store pulling outfits off the racks and tossing them over her arm. Then she headed for the dressing room.

"Wait!" called a saleswoman. "You dropped this blouse!"

"No time!" Jade shouted back. "I'll just try these, thanks!"

Jade slipped into one outfit after another until she finally found the perfect one. She added a rhinestone-studded pair of black shades and practiced a few air guitar moves in front of the three-way mirror. Even the buttoned-up saleslady had to smile.

"I think that one is absolutely divine," the saleswoman told her.

"Now this is what I call rockin'!" Jade agreed. "I'll take four of them."

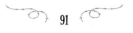

Laden with shopping bags, Jade headed back to the suite to find Sasha working out some dance moves in front of the mirror and Cloe and Yasmin hunched over pages and pages of lyrics and sheet music.

Jade plopped into a cushy chair and the shopping bags crashed around her feet. She groaned with exhaustion. "I am totally shopped out!" she declared. "But wait till you guys see the outfits I got us! You're going to love them!"

"All right, people!" Sasha announced. "I've got the moves down."

Yasmin and Cloe looked up from the music they were working on. They gave each other a high-five.

"Rock out!" Cloe said.

"We've got it!" Yasmin yelled. "Now we just have to put it all together."

The girls pulled the clothes out of the shopping bags and got dressed. Then Sasha taught everyone her dance moves, and Yasmin and Cloe recited the lyrics they had come up with.

"Rock on, Rock Angelz!" Sasha declared. "We're scorchin'!"

The girls high-fived.

"Wait a minute," Yasmin said. Something had dawned on her. "Aren't we missing something?"

The girls looked at one another uneasily.

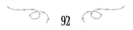

"We forgot the guitars!" Jade exclaimed.

"Oh my gosh!" Cloe gasped. "We'll never get them in time for the concert! The bouncer won't let us in, we won't get our backstage exclusive or interview with Byron Powell, our premiere issue of *Bratz Magazine* will tank, and I'll have to go camping with my parents and sing Elvis songs!"

As soon as Cloe had finished her outburst, Cameron and Dylan burst into the suite, each carrying two guitars.

"Hey, guys," Cameron said proudly. "Look what we scored at the flea market!" he and Dylan tossed a guitar to each girl. The instruments totally completed each girl's rock star look.

"Yes!" they shouted as they strummed their guitars and played a jamming riff, incorporating Sasha's scorchin' dance moves.

"Wow!" Cameron said, impressed.

"You guys rock!" Dylan confirmed.

"Man, I didn't know you girls could play guitars like that!" Cameron said.

Cloe smiled at him. "There are a lot of things you don't know about us," she said sweetly.

The phone in the suite jangled loudly.

"Got it!" Sasha announced as she sauntered over to the phone.

"Sasha here," she said into the receiver. "See you in a few."

She turned back to her friends as she hung up the phone. "Our limo is waiting."

"Limo?!" Jade asked. "Stylin'!"

"Slammin'!" Yasmin added.

"Rockin'!" Cloe shouted, giving Sasha a high five.

"People, it is time for the Bratz Rock Angelz to rock the world!" Sasha shouted.

Chapter Twelve

Yasmin, Cloe, Jade, and Sasha strutted confidently toward the bouncer. They had full-on rock star make-up on, and their outfits were rocked out to the max. Cameron trailed behind them, lugging the girls' guitars and some of the other audio equipment.

"Yo, Bratz Rock Angelz!" Dylan shouted at them. "Over here!"

He started snapping photos of the girls using a camera with an enormous flash.

"This one's for the cover of the premiere issue of *Bratz Magazine*!" Dylan announced loudly.

The girls put on their best rock star smiles and posed for the camera just as Burdine, Kirstee, and Kaycee came up behind them. Nigel was with them. He began to wander off into the crowd, and Kirstee dashed after him.

"Dukey!" She screeched. "Where are you going?"

"Oh, you know," he answered. "Just thought I'd venture out to sneer at the exploits of the masses."

Kirstee and Kaycee followed Nigel off into the crowd, leaving Burdine behind.

"Where's my entourage?" Burdine screamed.

Then she spotted Nigel. "Mother of pink!" she cried. "It's a *royal*!"

She elbowed her way through the crowd, shoving Kaycee out of the way.

"You're Nigel Forrester!" Burdine gushed. "The ninth Duke of Lessex! As I'm sure you know, I'm Burdine Maxwell, the founder, president, and editor-in-chief of *Your Thing* magazine, and the reigning queen of fashion."

Nigel looked at her scornfully. "Look, queen of whatever you are," he sneered. "Go find someone my father's age."

Burdine's jaw dropped. "Your *father's* age?"

Kaycee and Kirstee snickered in the background.

Meanwhile, the Bratz Rock Angelz were still at the door. Dylan's camera kept lighting up like a strobe light as he took one photo after another, blinding both the girls and the bouncer. Cameron and the girls continued walking toward the door as Dylan chased after them.

"Man, don't you recognize the Bratz Rock Angelz?" Dylan asked the bouncer. "They're the most stylin', hip new rock band around."

The bouncer looked down at his list.

"Keep Mr. Space Invader away from us, okay?!" Sasha said to the bouncer, gesturing toward Dylan. She and Dylan had a plan to get him into the club with the rest of them.

The bouncer nodded and stepped aside, opening the door for the girls and Cameron to walk through. Dylan continued snapping away, aiming the camera at the bouncer. The flash temporarily blinded the bouncer, and Dylan was able to slip past him.

The girls raced into the club and started looking around for Byron.

"We did it!" Jade shouted. "We're in!"

"Scorchin'!" Sasha replied. "Now let's scoop this concert."

Then the girls heard a voice behind them in the background.

"What do you mean, Crash crashed?" the voice asked. "The band broke up?!"

"Oh my gosh!" Cloe whispered to her friends. "That's Byron talking! C'mon!"

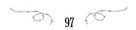

Cloe grabbed her friends and pulled them toward the voice, which was coming from a room off the main floor.

Byron was inside talking to Roxxi, the lead singer of Crash.

"Yeah, the band split," Roxxi told Byron. "It's over for Crash. But I'm not ready to go solo."

"This is absolutely, positively an unmitigated disaster!" Byron said. He slumped down in a chair.

"I know!" Roxxi agreed. "I feel terrible. This concert meant so much to everyone."

"Oh my gosh!" Cloe said. "You're Roxxi, the lead singer of Crash!"

Byron and Roxxi spun around to see the four girls standing in the doorway.

"Actually, that's 'formerly of Crash,'" Roxxi said wryly.

"Byron turned back to Roxxi. "You were supposed to go on stage *now*," he lamented. "What are we going to do?"

Roxxi looked at the girls. "Hey," she said. "Can you girls play?"

The girls played a rockin' riff on their guitars in response.

"Roxxi, get ready to rock out with the Bratz Rock Angelz," Sasha said confidently.

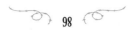

Byron stepped out onto the stage and the crowd roared.

"Are you ready?" Byron shouted into the microphone. There war a huge roar in response.

"The Save the Universe Benefit Concert welcomes . . . the Bratz Rock Angelz!"

The girls stepped out onto the stage in an explosion of fireworks.

Burdine and the Tweevils were standing in front of the stage. Their mouths dropped open.

"Those Bratz!" Burdine shrieked. "What are they doing up there?! Get down! Do you hear me? Get down!"

Burdine started to climb up onto the stage, but the bouncer quickly swooped in.

"Okay, lady," he said. "Let's go." He slung Burdine over his shoulder and carried her off.

"I'll have you arrested!" Burdine shouted as she pounded her fists on the bouncer's back. "Do you know who I am? Put me down!"

The Bratz Rock Angelz and Roxxi played to a packed house, and the crowd whistled and cheered in response. Just before they were about to step offstage, the girls turned to the audience.

"We love you!" they shouted into the microphone. There was a huge cheer. "Thank you, everyone!"

Then they turned and exited the stage in the midst of a flurry of fireworks and camera flashes.

Chapter Thirteen

Six weeks later, the girls were back at home in the *Bratz Magazine* office, busy working on their second issue. Jade was pinning clothes on a mannequin, Sasha was rockin' out with her headphones on and making occasional notes on a pad of paper as she bopped to the beat, and Cloe was working on a layout. Yasmin sat at the computer, typing away.

"Can you guys believe we launched our very own teen magazine, got a free trip to London, *and* became rock stars?!" Cloe mused.

"That trip to London gave us so many awesome stories, guys," Jade said with a sigh.

"Yeah, like our exclusive celebrity interview with Byron Powell, the ultimate judge," Yasmin added. "I can't believe he told us we were absolutely, positively the best band he had *ever* heard!"

"And our first issue of *Bratz Magazine* has been a

huge success!" Sasha added. "Which means we have to start thinking about our next one, pronto."

"I'm thinking of my very own dos and don'ts column," Jade mused. She imagined her friends' styles in the "do" column, and the awful Tweevils in the "don't" category.

Suddenly, Jade thought of something she hadn't told her friends.

"Did I ever tell you guys that the week our magazine went on sale, I saw Burdine in the building cafeteria, eating a burger with extra cheese and mayo?!" Jade asked.

"No way!" Sasha gasped.

"She looked so depressed, I almost felt bad for her," Jade said. "But then I overheard her blaming everything on the Tweevils, and I didn't feel so bad. I heard she has them working round-the-clock cleaning her office and her house to make up for it!"

"Those girls totally deserve it," Yasmin added.

Cloe nodded in agreement. "And they are going to flip when they hear about the Bratz Rock Angelz world tour, coming up in a few weeks," she said.

"What a summer," Yasmin sighed, leaning back in her chair. "I don't think we'll ever have another one like it. Will we, girls?"

The girls looked at one another and shrugged.

"You never know!" Sasha replied. "But I think we should definitely celebrate our success right now with a little impromptu dance party."

"Right now?" Cloe asked.

"Right here?" Jade asked, gesturing to the office around them.

"Why not?" Sasha replied, turning on the boom box. "We deserve a little break from work."

Jade, Cloe, and Yasmin jumped out of their chairs. "Awesome idea, Bunny Boo!" they chimed together.

The song playing on the radio faded out and the announcer's voice came on.

"And our countdown continues with the new number-one hit from the Bratz Rock Angelz!"

"Our song!" Jade cried.

"We're number one!" Cloe squealed with delight.

"Scorchin'!" Sasha added.

"Slammin'!" Yasmin agreed.

The girls danced to their song like the rock stars they were. It had been an incredible summer, and they weren't going to forget it—ever.

**NOW, TAKE A LOOK INSIDE THE
BRATZ GIRLS' VERY OWN MAGAZINE!**

Rockin' Room

BY SASHA

Aside from school, your room is probably where you spend most of your time, right?

Every stylin' girl knows that her room is her own special space, and it should reflect her individual personality. Chances are, you're not exactly the same girl you were five years ago, and if your room still looks the same as it did then, it may be time for a change. Time for the three *R*s—redo, redesign, and rearrange.

Redo: Pick one thing in your room that you'd love to change completely. Ask an adult for permission, and then go to it! Maybe you want to paint your walls a fresh, funky color like fuchsia or lavender. Or maybe you want to make your own curtains out of some sparkly fabric to give your windows a whole new look.

Rockin' Room Redo!

. . . cont'd

Redesign: Pick a color scheme and redesign your space around it. Colors that go well together include red and purple, blue and purple, pink and red, green and blue, and yellow and purple. A blanket in one color and a few accessories (picture frames, shimmery lamp shades, and beaded pillows are good ones!) or curtains in the complementary color could be all it takes to pull it all together.

Rearrange: This is the easy part—just move things around! Maybe your bed's been under the window for years. Try moving your desk under the window instead—the sunlight may even make it easier to study! Or try angling your bed out into the room from a corner. This will definitely mix things up a bit, and it can help make a small room look larger.

Is Your Boyfriend a Royal Jerk?

BY CLOE

He may seem like a real Prince Charming, but he could be a royal jerk in disguise. Take this slammin' quiz to find out!

1. He likes to call you by a nickname of his own invention, and you really don't like it. When you tell him, he:

a. Apologizes and immediately stops using the name.

b. Teases you about it, but eventually gives up using it.

c. Is too busy with his own thing to notice you're talking to him.

Is Your Boyfriend a Royal Jerk?

. . . cont'd

2. You have a date with him on Friday. On Thursday night he calls to:

a. Ask if you would mind meeting him at the restaurant—he has a few things to do beforehand and can't pick you up as planned.

b. Confirm the time and place where he'll be picking you up.

c. Cancel without rescheduling.

3. He hates your favorite song. Whenever it plays on the radio, he:

a. Immediately switches to another station.

b. Turns the volume up and jokingly belts it out for you.

c. Groans and complains about how much he hates it.

4.

On your birthday, he:

a. Is late for your date but makes up for it with a sweet homemade card.

b. Tells you he owes you a present.

c. Surprises you at your locker with flowers and a crown that makes you "Queen for the Day."

5.

It's the night of the big dance, and you're sick with the flu. He:

a. Calls to say sorry you're sick, but he's gotta go meet his friends.

b. Stops by on his way to and from the dance, bringing you your corsage.

c. Stays behind to decorate your room with balloons and streamers. Then he turns on the radio and asks you to dance with him even though you're in your pajamas.

Is Your Boyfriend a Royal Jerk?

. . . cont'd

Answers:

1. a) 3 b) 2 c) 1   **2.** a) 2 b) 3 c) 1 **3.** a) 1 b) 3 c) 2

4. a) 2 b) 1 c) 3   **5.** a) 1 b) 2 c) 3

12-15: Divine Duke

It looks like you may have found your knight in shining armor. This guy is a real sweetie—he's caring and treats you right. Most importantly, he probably respects you a lot and considers you one of his closest friends in addition to being his girlfriend.

9-12: Borderline Royalty

This prince-in-training means well but occasionally falls short of the throne. Though he's sometimes a bit rough around the edges, this guy could be a hidden gem. Give him some time, and don't be afraid to speak up if you feel like he isn't giving you the time and attention that you deserve.

8 or below: Total Dud

This guy may look royal on the outside, but he's got a lot of work to do before he's a real prince. He may not realize that he's not taking your thoughts or opinions into consideration, but that's no excuse. You deserve to be treated like the queen that you are!

Pretty in PunK

BY JADE & YASMIN

Ever wonder how you can get that totally glam rock-star look? Check out these tips from the Bratz Rock Angelz for the 411 on making yourself look pretty in punk.

✩✩✩✩✩✩✩✩✩✩✩✩✩✩✩✩✩✩✩✩✩✩✩✩

make-up: Try some glitzy glam silver eye shadow and dark black eyeliner for a totally punkalish look! Don't forget to use a blush or toner with some shimmer in it. Your lipstick should be bright and dark so that the crowds of people can see it while you're up on stage. And don't forget a shiny lip gloss to finish off your glamorous, rock-star look!

✩✩✩✩✩✩✩✩✩✩✩✩✩✩✩✩✩✩✩✩✩✩✩✩

Hair: If your hair is naturally curly, consider blowing it pin straight. Then pull it up in a half-ponytail on the side of your head for a look that's punk, glam, and totally retro! If you have straight hair naturally, you can try this, too. Or you can put your hair up in pigtails and spike them with some hair gel or hair wax for a totally hot look! They even make colored hair waxes that will wash out, so why not give them one a try? Purple, red, fuchsia, or silver are perfect rock star colors!

Clothes: They say that clothes make the girl, and if you've got a passion for fashion, you know it's true! A funky T-shirt and a miniskirt are perfect for an aspiring rock star. Pair them with some brightly colored tights and some tall boots, and you've got a look that's totally slammin'! Don't forget the accessories—dangling earrings and a rhinestone-studded belt will complete the look.

NOW get glam and get out there and rock it, girl!